Dear Parent:
Your child's love of reading starts here!

Every child learns to read in a different way and at his or her own speed. Some go back and forth between reading levels and read favorite books again and again. Others read through each level in order. You can help your young reader improve and become more confident by encouraging his or her own interests and abilities. From books your child reads with you to the first books he or she reads alone, there are I Can Read Books for every stage of reading:

SHARED READING
Basic language, word repetition, and whimsical illustrations, ideal for sharing with your emergent reader

BEGINNING READING
Short sentences, familiar words, and simple concepts for children eager to read on their own

READING WITH HELP
Engaging stories, longer sentences, and language play for developing readers

READING ALONE
Complex plots, challenging vocabulary, and high-interest topics for the independent reader

ADVANCED READING
Short paragraphs, chapters, and exciting themes for the perfect bridge to chapter books

I Can Read Books have introduced children to the joy of reading since 1957. Featuring award-winning authors and illustrators and a fabulous cast of beloved characters, I Can Read Books set the standard for beginning readers.

A lifetime of discovery begins with the magical words "I Can Read!"

Visit www.icanread.com for information
on enriching your child's reading experience.

For
Susan Hirschman,
who's been with me
all the way,
with love

Watercolors and a black pen were used for the full-color art.

HarperCollins®, ☙®, and I Can Read Book® are trademarks of HarperCollins Publishers Inc.

Library of Congress Cataloging-in-Publication Data

Parish, Peggy.
   Amelia Bedelia's family album / by Peggy Parish ; pictures by Lynn Sweat.
      p.   cm.—(An I can read book)
   "Greenwillow Books"
   Summary: Amelia Bedelia entertains Mr. and Mrs. Rogers by showing them her family album and describing what her relatives do.
   ISBN-10: 0-688-07676-9 (trade bdg.) — ISBN-13: 978-0-688-07676-4 (trade bdg.)
   ISBN-10: 0-06-051116-8 (pbk.) — ISBN-13: 978-0-06-051116-6 (pbk.)
   [1. Family—Fiction. 2. Humorous stories.] I. Sweat, Lynn, ill. II. Title. III. Series.
PZ7.P219 Aq 1998   87-15641
[Fic]—dc19   CIP
                                                                                                                    AC

❖   Originally published by Greenwillow Books, an imprint of HarperCollins Publishers, in 1988.

I Can Read!

Amelia Bedelia's Family Album

by Peggy Parish

pictures by Lynn Sweat

HarperCollins*Publishers*

"Amelia Bedelia," said Mrs. Rogers, "you have been here a long time."

"Oh, Mrs. Rogers," said Amelia Bedelia, "are you tired of me?"

"Of course not," said Mrs. Rogers.

We want to have a party for you.

Ve want to meet your family."

Now that is nice," said Amelia Bedelia.

Who would you like to invite?"

sked Mrs. Rogers.

"I'll get my family album,"
said Amelia Bedelia.

"You can help me decide."

"Good idea," said Mr. Rogers.

Amelia Bedelia got her album.

"This is my mama," said Amelia Bedelia. "She is a loafer."

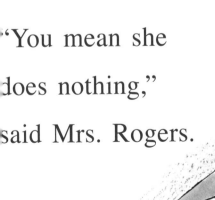

"You mean she does nothing," said Mrs. Rogers.

"Certainly not," said Amelia Bedelia. "She works hard. She makes dough into loaves of bread. That's what a loafer does."

"I see," said Mrs. Rogers.

'This is Uncle Albert,"

said Amelia Bedelia.

'He is a big-game hunter."

'You mean

he kills animals?"

asked Mrs. Rogers.

"Why would he do that?"

said Amelia Bedelia.

"He hunts big games.

He has one so big

it takes up a whole room."

"I see," said Mrs. Rogers.

12

"Next is Aunt Mary,"
said Amelia Bedelia.
"She is a bank teller."

"Then she cashes
people's checks,"
said Mr. Rogers.

"No," said Amelia Bedelia,
"she tells everybody
in the bank
where to go.
Some folks don't like that."
"I see," said Mr. Rogers.

"This is Cousin Calvin," said Amelia Bedelia. "He is a boxer."

"Does he win any matches?" asked Mrs. Rogers.

Amelia Bedelia looked puzzled.

"Matches!" she said.

"Why would he win matches?

A boxer packs boxes.

He gets paid money."

"I see," said Mrs. Rogers.

"Cousin Edward
is a horse racer,"
said Amelia Bedelia.
"Oh, he is a jockey,"
said Mr. Rogers.

"I don't think so," said Amelia Bedelia.

"Cousin Edward races horses.

He almost won once.

But he tripped and fell."

"I see," said Mr. Rogers.

"Uncle Ned is a Cook,"

said Amelia Bedelia.

"He works in a hotel."

"Then he is a chef,"

said Mrs. Rogers.

"No," said Amelia Bedelia.

"He is a doorman.

His name is Ned Cook."

"I see," said Mrs. Rogers.

"Uncle Dan takes pictures,"
said Amelia Bedelia.
"What kind of pictures
does he take?" asked Mr. Rogers.

"Any kind," said Amelia Bedelia.
"You really have to watch him.
He will take every picture
in the house."
"I see," said Mr. Rogers.

"Cousin Bea has a fun job," said Amelia Bedelia. "She balances checkbooks."

"I wish she would balance mine," said Mrs. Rogers.

"She will," said Amelia Bedelia.

"She can balance twenty at one time."

"I see," said Mrs. Rogers.

"My brother Ike
wants an orange grove,"
said Amelia Bedelia,
"but he has had bad luck."

"How is that?"
asked Mr. Rogers.

25

"He orders orange trees,"
said Amelia Bedelia,
"but they all come out green."
"I see," said Mr. Rogers.

"This is poor Cousin Chester,"

said Amelia Bedelia.

"He is a printer."

"What does he print?"

asked Mrs. Rogers.

"Everything," said Amelia Bedelia.
"We could never teach him
proper writing."
"I see," said Mrs. Rogers.

"Cousin Clara is a bookkeeper,"
said Amelia Bedelia.

"She must be good with numbers,"
said Mr. Rogers.

"No," said Amelia Bedelia.

"But she is good at keeping books.

She never returns one."

"I see," said Mr. Rogers.

"Cousin Ella works with Clay," said Amelia Bedelia.

"Is she a potter?" asked Mrs. Rogers.
"I don't know any Potters," said Amelia Bedelia.

"Ella and her husband, Clay,
have a bakery," said
Amelia Bedelia.
"I see," said Mrs. Rogers.

"Uncle Alf is a garbage collector,"

said Amelia Bedelia.

"That is smelly work,"

said Mr. Rogers.

"It sure is," said Amelia Bedelia.

"All of his neighbors moved away."

"I see," said Mr. Rogers.

"Cousin Susan belongs to
a fan club," said Amelia Bedelia.
"Are there many fans in her club?"
asked Mr. Rogers.

"Oh yes," said Amelia Bedelia.
"You never saw so many
different kinds of fans."
"I see," said Mr. Rogers.

My niece Lulu
tuffs olives,"
aid Amelia Bedelia.

"Does she stuff the pimento
in the middle?"
asked Mrs. Rogers.

"No," said Amelia Bedelia,
"she stuffs olives into herself."
"I see," said Mrs. Rogers.

"The last picture
s of Ollie,"
aid Amelia Bedelia.
"He is my nephew.
Ollie is our catcher."

"What does he catch?" asked Mr. Rogers.

"Everything," said Amelia Bedelia.
"Measles, mumps, colds.
Whatever comes along,
Ollie catches it."

"What an unusual family,"
said Mrs. Rogers.

"Yes," said Mr. Rogers.

"Invite all of them to the party."

"All right," said Amelia Bedelia.

She left the room.

n a bit she came back.

They will be here tomorrow," she said.

Tomorrow!" said Mrs. Rogers.

We can't get everything ready by then."

What's to get ready?"

sked Amelia Bedelia.

Food!" said Mr. Rogers.

"Now, Mr. Rogers," said Amelia Bedelia,

"my folks know about parties.

They will bring the food."

"But Amelia Bedelia," said Mrs. Rogers,

"will there be enough food

for everybody?"

"Everybody!" said Amelia Bedelia.

"I hadn't thought of inviting everybody.

What a good idea!"

She ran outside.

"Hear! Hear!" she shouted.

"A party tomorrow.

Everybody come."

And everybody came!